SADIQ
and the
Green Thumbs

BY SIMAN NUURALI

ART BY ANJAN SARKAR

PICTURE WINDOW BOOKS
a capstone imprint

Sadiq is published by Picture Window Books,
a Capstone imprint
1710 Roe Crest Drive
North Mankato, Minnesota 56003
www.mycapstone.com

Library of Congress Cataloging-in-Publication Data
Names: Nuurali, Siman, author. | Sarkar, Anjan, illustrator.
Title: Sadiq and the Green Thumbs / by Siman Nuurali ; illustrated by Anjan
   Sarkar.
Description: North Mankato, Minnesota : Picture Window Books, [2019] |
   Series: Sadiq | Summary: Even though it is summer Sadiq goes to religious
   school four days a week to study the Quran; he and his friends find their
   teacher, Mr. Kassim, strict and intimidating, but when Sadiq finds out
   that Mr. Kassim has an injured shoulder he decides to volunteer to help
   with the gardening—and he convinces his friends to volunteer as well.
Identifiers: LCCN 2018052128| ISBN 9781515838791 (hardcover) | ISBN
   9781515845676 (pbk.) | ISBN 9781515838838 (ebook pdf)
Subjects: LCSH: Muslim families—Juvenile fiction. | Children of
   immigrants—Juvenile fiction. | Africans—United States—Juvenile fiction.
   | Helping behavior—Juvenile fiction. | Islamic education—Juvenile
   fiction. | Teachers—Juvenile fiction. | Gardening—Juvenile fiction. |
   CYAC: Muslims—United States—Fiction. | Immigrants—Fiction. |
   Africans—United States—Fiction. | Helpfulness—Fiction. | Islamic
   education—Fiction. | Teachers—Fiction. | Gardening—Fiction.
Classification: LCC PZ7.1.N9 Sah 2019 | DDC [Fic]—dc23
LC record available at https://lccn.loc.gov/2018052128

Designer: Brann Garvey
Design Element: Shutterstock/Irtsya

TABLE OF CONTENTS

FACTS ABOUT SOMALIA

- Most Somali people belong to one of four major groups: the Darod, Isaaq, Hawiye, and Dir.
- Many Somalis are nomadic. That means they travel from place to place. They search for water, food, and land for their animals.
- Somalia is mostly desert. It doesn't rain often there.
- The camel is an important animal to Somali people. Camels can survive a long time without food or water.
- Around ninety-nine percent of all Somalis are Muslim.

SOMALI TERMS

ayah (AYE-yah)—verse

baba (BAH-baah)—a common word for father

cashar (AAHSH-ar)—an Arabic term for lesson

habo (HAA-bo)—aunt; or a term for a Somali woman

hooyo (HOY-yoh)—mother

kufi (COO-fee)—a close-fitting round hat

ma'alin (MAH-leen)—teacher

salaam (sa-LAHM)—a short form of Arabic greeting, used by many Muslims. It also means "peace." The longer versions of the greeting are *as-salaamu alaykum* and *wa-alaykuma salaam*.

CHAPTER 1

SADIQ GOES TO DUGSI

"Sadiq!" Hooyo called up the stairs. "Please hurry up or we'll be late for Dugsi. We have to pick up Zaza on the way."

Sadiq's mother checked to make sure her hijab was secured properly with a pin.

"I'm coming, Hooyo," said Sadiq, running down the stairs. He didn't want to be late for Qur'an school. "I was just looking for my *kufi.*"

It was summer and school was out, but Sadiq still had to attend Dugsi four days a week to learn the Qur'an.

"How does it always get lost?" asked Hooyo. She shook her head and smiled.

"I don't know, Hooyo. But I always find it!" Sadiq said. Kufis were small hats he wore for Dugsi. He had three, but they were always falling behind his bed or getting lost in his clothes.

"Why are we giving Zaza a ride?" Sadiq asked while he tied his shoes.

"Faiza's car broke down," Hooyo said as they headed out to the driveway. "She had to get it towed to the auto shop. They live close by, so I said I would be happy to give Zaza a ride."

"That's nice of you, Hooyo," said
Sadiq. He got into the car and buckled
his seat belt.

Soon they got to Zaza's house. He
was standing outside waiting for them
with his mom.

"Bye, Hooyo," Zaza said, waving as
he walked to the car.

"Thanks again, Samiya," said Faiza.
"You've saved me!"

"Anytime, Faiza," said Hooyo,
waving out the window of the car.
"It's no trouble at all."

* * *

Sadiq and Zaza walked into the
classroom just ahead of their teacher,
Mr. Kassim.

Sadiq was a little afraid of Mr. Kassim. Last week, Mr. Kassim had glared at Sadiq when he forgot his *ayahs.* That only made it harder for Sadiq to remember them!

The other students were already sitting down with their Qur'ans open. Zaza and Sadiq slid into seats on either side of their friend Manny.

"*As-salaamu alaykum,* children," said Mr. Kassim.

"*Wa-alaykuma salaam, Ma'alin,*" replied all the kids at once.

"Before we get started, I have a quick announcement to make," Mr. Kassim said as he stood in front of the class.

"After class, a carpenter is coming to put in new storage cupboards for the classroom," Mr. Kassim said. "I'll need a few students to stay behind and roll up all the prayer mats. I hurt my shoulder over the weekend, so I can't do it on my own."

Sadiq looked down at his Qur'an. He didn't really want to stay behind.

"Are you going to volunteer?" Manny whispered.

Sadiq shook his head. "I'm supposed to go biking with Nuurali when I get home."

"Does everyone remember their *cashar* from last week?" Mr. Kassim interrupted before Manny could reply.

"Yes," all the students replied.

"Okay, let's start with you, Hashim," said Mr. Kassim. "Come up here and recite your cashar."

Everyone turned to their Qur'ans to do some last-minute reading, but Sadiq couldn't help thinking about his mom helping *Habo* Faiza that morning. He knew helping people in times of need was the right thing to do. But he really wanted to go for a bike ride!

CHAPTER 2

A GROCERY TRIP

Later that day, after Sadiq and Nuurali went biking, they helped Baba go grocery shopping. As they got out of the car, Nuurali peered across the Big Foods parking lot. "Isn't that your ma'alin from Dugsi, Sadiq?" he asked.

"You're right, Nuurali," said Baba as they walked toward the store entrance. "That's Mr. Kassim. Why is he moving so slowly?"

"His shoulder must still be hurting," said Sadiq. "He told us about it today."

"Let's help him put his groceries in the car. He shouldn't lift heavy items if he's injured," said Baba. He walked toward Mr. Kassim.

"*Salaam,* Kassim!" Baba called. "Sadiq tells me you hurt your shoulder. Let me get that for you." He picked up some bags from the cart. Then he placed them in the trunk of Mr. Kassim's car.

"Salaam, Mohammed," said Mr. Kassim. "That's very nice of you. Thank you! It's not too bad, really." He frowned a little.

Nuurali joined Baba. He moved two bags from the cart to Mr. Kassim's car. Then he took the cart to the corral.

"What happened?" asked Baba.

"I was reaching for a flashlight I keep in the top kitchen cabinet. Suddenly I felt a sharp pain in my shoulder," said Mr. Kassim. "It's been hurting ever since."

"You should be at home resting!" said Baba.

"My wife traveled to Somalia last week to care for her mom who is sick, and I needed to get groceries," said Mr. Kassim. "I wanted to do some gardening and other chores around the house, but I wasn't able to because of my shoulder injury. This I can do on my own, at least!"

"You should see a doctor if it continues to bother you, Kassim. You wouldn't want to hurt yourself even more," said Baba. "Have a nice day. Let us know if you need anything."

"Thanks!" said Mr. Kassim as he waved goodbye to Sadiq and his family.

As Nuurali, Baba, and Sadiq went into the store to shop, Sadiq was quiet.

He thought about his mother helping Habo Faiza when she needed it. He also thought about Baba and Nuurali helping Mr. Kassim put his groceries into his car. *I probably should have helped Mr. Kassim with the mats,* he thought. He felt bad for his teacher, and also a little guilty.

After they got home, Nuurali put away the groceries. Sadiq asked his mom if he could go play outside. He knew he should help Nuurali, but Sadiq didn't like doing chores. He would much rather play soccer or video games!

"Yes, but only for a half hour or so," said Hooyo. "It's almost time for dinner."

Sadiq hurried outside. Zaza and Manny were already in the park, kicking a soccer ball.

"I saw Mr. Kassim at the grocery store," said Sadiq.

"Ugh, Mr. Kassim is mean," said Zaza. "I'm still mad at him for making us stay behind last weekend and do extra cashar."

"He told my mom. She took away video games for a week," said Manny. He made a face. "If you hadn't made me laugh in class, Zaza, we could be playing the new *Space Sprinter* now!"

"Maybe we should help him, though," Sadiq said. "He's hurt, and his wife is away for a long time."

Manny and Zaza frowned and shook their heads.

"He doesn't need our help," Manny said. "I bet he's got friends who can help him."

"C'mon, guys!" Zaza said. "It will be dark soon. Let's see if we can get a soccer game in before then." He ran toward another group of kids down the field, kicking his soccer ball ahead of him.

CHAPTER 3

SADIQ OFFERS TO HELP

The next morning, Sadiq and Nuurali were in their room getting ready to go downstairs for breakfast.

"Are you playing soccer with Zaza and Manny later?" asked Nuurali.

"I'm not sure yet," replied Sadiq. "Mr. Kassim might give us extra cashar."

"He looked like he was in pain yesterday. Maybe he'll let you out early," said Nuurali.

"I felt sorry for him," said Sadiq. "He didn't look as mean as he usually does."

"Are you sure it's not his bushy eyebrows?" asked Nuurali. He tried to make a scary face.

"Haha, very funny," said Sadiq. He stuck his tongue out.

"Anyway, he could probably use some help in the class or even at home," said Nuurali. "Yesterday he said that he wanted to garden."

"Should I offer to help him?" asked Sadiq.

"I think that would be a nice thing to do, Sadiq," replied Nuurali. "Let's go downstairs. You can talk to Baba and Hooyo about it."

Sadiq looked up to Nuurali and thought he was the smartest brother in the world!

If Nuurali thinks I should help Mr. Kassim, it must be the right thing to do, Sadiq thought.

The brothers headed downstairs for breakfast. As they sat down at the table to eat with their family, Sadiq spoke up. "Baba. Hooyo," he said. "I was thinking of helping Mr. Kassim. I wanted to make sure it was okay with you."

"That's a very nice thing to do, Sadiq!" said Baba.

"Of course you can help him, Sadiq. We should always try to help others if we can," said Hooyo.

"What will you help him with?" Baba asked.

"He mentioned needing help with his garden," said Sadiq. "Hooyo, could we go to his house after Dugsi?"

"Yes, that will be fine," said his mother.

* * *

During class at Dugsi, Sadiq thought about how to offer Mr. Kassim his help.

What if he says no, or doesn't think I know how to garden? thought Sadiq. *He might think I am offering to help to get out of cashar.*

When class ended, Sadiq took a deep breath and walked to the front of the classroom.

"Salaam, Sadiq. Did you forget something?" asked Mr. Kassim.

"Salaam, Ma'alin," said Sadiq. "No, I didn't forget anything. I just wanted to see if you needed help with your garden. I know you hurt your shoulder. It must be hard to garden when you're in pain."

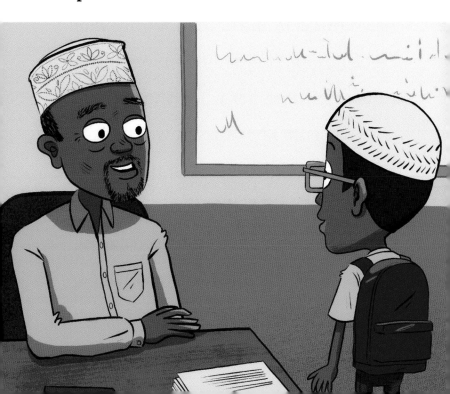

Mr. Kassim looked surprised. "That is very kind, Sadiq," he said. "Did you ask your parents?"

"Yes, Ma'alin," replied Sadiq. "They said it was fine as long as it was okay with you."

"It's really nice of you to offer, Sadiq," said Mr. Kassim. "I did want to plant new flowers in the garden for my wife. I was hoping they would bloom just in time to surprise her when she returns."

"I am sure Mrs. Kassim would like that. They might cheer her up when she gets back," said Sadiq.

After Mr. Kassim had locked up, he and Sadiq walked outside together. Hooyo was waiting in the parking lot.

Sadiq ran toward Hooyo's car. "See you at your house!" he called to Mr. Kassim.

A few minutes later, Sadiq and Hooyo arrived at Mr. Kassim's. They walked up to his front door, and Sadiq pushed the doorbell.

"Salaam, Kassim!" Hooyo said when Mr. Kassim came to the door. "How are you feeling?"

"Salaam, Samiya. I am still sore, but I'm thankful that Sadiq has very kindly offered to help," said Mr. Kassim as he invited them in. "I already bought the soil and seeds and other supplies before I hurt my shoulder, but I haven't been able to do anything."

"Don't worry, Mr. Kassim. We'll have the garden ready when Mrs. Kassim comes back," said Sadiq.

"Let's take a look at the yard," said Mr. Kassim as he led them toward the back of the house. "I can show you where to plant the flowers."

As they walked outside, Sadiq looked around. "It's a really big yard!" he said. He was expecting something smaller.

Sadiq got to work planting some potted marigolds Mr. Kassim had on his porch. While Sadiq worked, Mr. Kassim and Hooyo caught up with each other. They sat on the deck and chatted while they drank coffee.

Sadiq dug and planted, dug and planted, until the marigolds were all in the ground. It seemed like it had taken hours! But the garden still needed work. There was plenty of empty space that needed to be planted. He was going to need help—a lot of help!

"I finished planting the marigolds, Mr. Kassim!" Sadiq called.

"It looks wonderful, Sadiq," Mr. Kassim said. He looked out from the deck.

"Is it okay if I ask my friends to help with the rest?" asked Sadiq. "I'm sure they'd like to help with the surprise! We could come back tomorrow since we don't have Dugsi."

"Sure," said Mr. Kassim, smiling. "Thanks, both of you. It's very kind of you to let him come over to help, Samiya."

"You're welcome, Kassim," replied Hooyo. "What are neighbors for?" She smiled.

"No problem, Mr. Kassim!" said Sadiq. He waved goodbye as they walked to the car.

"I hope I can get Zaza and Manny to help me," said Sadiq to his mother.

"Well, I just got a text from your Baba. Guess who's waiting at home for you?" said Hooyo.

CHAPTER 4

PLANTING THE GARDEN

As Hooyo pulled into the driveway, Sadiq spotted Zaza and Manny waiting on the front porch. He hurried out of the car to fill them in on his idea to help Mr. Kassim. They did not seem excited about the possibility.

"Come on, guys," said Sadiq. "I really need your help. We would be doing a nice thing for Mr. Kassim. We could even make it a club!"

"But Mr. Kassim is so crabby!" said
Zaza. "He's always frowning. I don't
think I've ever seen him smile."

"I'm still mad at him for making me
stay behind last week," said Manny.

"If you help, I'll let each of you borrow
Jungle Trek for a week," said Sadiq.

Zaza and Manny looked at each other and grinned. A whole week!

"Okay, we'll help," said Zaza.

"Sure thing, buddy," said Manny, putting his arm around Sadiq's shoulder. "Gardening Club, here we come!"

"Yeah!" shouted Sadiq. Gardening would be a lot more fun with his friends there to help.

* * *

The next day, the boys went over to Mr. Kassim's to help with his garden.

"The first thing to do is decide where we want to plant and put some markers in the ground so we don't mistake them for weeds," said Mr. Kassim.

"How do we decide where to plant?" asked Sadiq.

"It's important for these flowers to have plenty of light so they can grow," said Mr. Kassim. "I think this sunny corner of the yard would be best."

"What are we planting?" asked Manny.

"Sunflowers and morning glories," said Mr. Kassim. He picked up a tray of seedlings from the porch. They were small and didn't have flowers yet. "They are Mrs. Kassim's favorite. They're easy to grow as long as they have sunlight and water."

"How come they're her favorite flowers?" asked Sadiq.

"She loves the colors," said Mr. Kassim. "Purple and yellow are her favorites. Now, let's start by digging holes for the seedlings. We should mark the rows so we remember where we planted them. Then we can begin planting."

The boys got to work spreading the soil evenly. Then they began digging holes for the seedlings and marking the rows. As they dug, they found worms wriggling in the soil. Manny held one up in front of Zaza. The boys all laughed. Gardening was actually fun!

After a while, Mr. Kassim brought out lemonade for them. "Come and take a break," he said.

"Thank you for the lemonade," said Sadiq. "It's really tasty!"

"You're welcome!" Mr. Kassim said. "You know, I used to help my hooyo with her garden when I was a little boy. She didn't let anyone touch the flowers, but she did let me water them for her."

Sadiq could not imagine Mr. Kassim as a little boy!

"Did she like flowers too?" asked Zaza.

"Oh, yes!" said Mr. Kassim. "She liked to relax in her garden after a long day because the flowers smelled so nice!"

Just then, they heard voices. "Hi, you guys! Hi, Mr. Kassim!" Walter and Gavin walked into the yard.

The boys lived across the street
from Mr. Kassim and went to the same
school as Sadiq, Zaza, and Manny.

"Hello, boys," Mr. Kassim said.
"What are you two up to?"

"We saw everyone helping, and it
looks like you're having fun. Is it okay
if we help, Mr. Kassim?" asked Walter.

"Yes, of course you can help," said
Mr. Kassim, smiling.

"We're just about to start planting
some seedlings," Sadiq said as he
finished his lemonade.

"We'll do one row of sunflowers
and one row of morning glories. Then
we'll repeat until we run out of room,"
explained Manny.

"Awesome," said Gavin.

"My hooyo says people who are good at gardening have 'green thumbs,'" said Zaza.

"Maybe we should call ourselves the Green Thumbs Club!" said Walter.

"I like that!" said Sadiq. "I'm setting the next meeting of the Green Thumbs Club for next Saturday afternoon. We'll come here after lunch to help water and weed. Does that work, Mr. Kassim?"

"Perfect! I'll take some help from the Green Thumbs Club any day!" he said, smiling, as the boys got to work planting the seedlings.

CHAPTER 5

A BUNNY IN THE GARDEN

When the boys came back the next weekend, they were hoping to see some flowers on the seedlings they'd planted. There were a few, but Mr. Kassim had some bad news! A bunny had gotten into the garden. It had eaten some of the flower shoots.

"Ugh," said Gavin. "They were eaten before they even bloomed?"

Mr. Kassim nodded sadly.

"What are we going to do?" asked
Walter.

"I'm not sure," said Sadiq. "Could
we put up a fence?"

"Good idea. Maybe we can make it,"
said Manny.

"Let's go and see if we can find
anything in Mr. Kassim's garage that
we can use," said Zaza.

"Good idea, Zaza," Mr. Kassim said.
He led them to the garage and opened
up the door.

The boys started looking around
slowly.

"How about these?" asked Sadiq.
He pointed to two pieces of wood
resting against the wall.

"I think we would need more than two pieces," said Gavin.

"What are these metal wires?" asked Walter.

"That's chicken wire," said Mr. Kassim. "I'll have to cut it for you so you don't hurt yourselves, but it would make a good fence. Why don't you boys go measure the garden plot to see how much fencing we'll need?" Mr. Kassim handed the boys a measuring tape.

"Sounds good, Mr. Kassim!" Sadiq said, taking the measuring tape. They walked back out into the yard.

Sadiq and Zaza measured the garden while Gavin wrote down the measurements.

They were careful not to step on the small shoots that still sprouted from the ground.

When they had finished measuring each side, the boys took the numbers to Mr. Kassim. He was ready with a pair of pliers and chicken wire.

"We'll have to put stakes in the ground to hold up the wire," said Mr. Kassim. "Every few inches, we'll hammer one into the ground through the chicken wire. My shoulder has been feeling a bit better. I should be able to do that if you boys can help hold up the fence."

The Green Thumbs Club agreed this was the best plan.

Walter and Manny held the wire up while Mr. Kassim hammered the stakes into the ground. The soil was soft so it wasn't hard to do. Soon they were done.

"There!" said Zaza. "Let's see Mr. Bunny try and get through that!"

They all laughed as they admired the new fence.

"Hello, boys!" someone called from the yard next door.

"Hi there!" said Mr. Kassim. "This is my neighbor, Mrs. Summers," he explained to the boys.

"It's very nice to meet you all," Mrs. Summers said. "I have been admiring your handiwork on Mr. Kassim's garden."

"We would love to help you, too, if you have any gardening projects!" Sadiq said.

"Hmm," Mrs. Summers said. "I could use some help picking the berries from the blueberry bushes in my yard. I have to stay in this wheelchair until my leg heals. I can't quite get to the berries!"

The boys all looked at each other and grinned.

"We'd love to help you!" Zaza said.

"Yum!" said Sadiq.

"I love blueberries," said Walter.

"Wonderful! When you're done at Mr. Kassim's, you can each pick some to bring home to your families," Mrs. Summers said.

"I think we're done here for the day," said Mr. Kassim. "Feel free to wash up and head next door to pick some berries!"

"Great!" said Sadiq. "Can we come back tomorrow to water the flowers and check on the fence?"

"That works for me!" said Mr. Kassim.

The boys washed their hands off with the hose. Then they walked next door to Mrs. Summers's yard.

Mrs. Summers gave each boy a bucket, and they started picking the berries.

"Look how blue my fingers are!" said Zaza.

"Mine look purple!" said Manny.

"I hope it washes off. Otherwise we'll turn everything we touch blue and purple!" said Walter, laughing.

The boys picked two bushes before they had to stop and go home. They each took a bowl of berries with them.

"Thanks, Mrs. Summers. We can help pick more berries tomorrow if you'd like!" said Sadiq.

"That's very kind of you," said Mrs. Summers.

"Thanks for the berries!" the boys all shouted.

* * *

The next day the Green Thumbs Club was at Mr. Kassim's watering the garden.

"Be careful with the water, Sadiq," said Mr. Kassim. "Too much water can be bad for the flowers."

Sadiq poured slower with the watering can, being careful to make it even.

Walter and Gavin pulled weeds from the dirt.

Zaza and Manny inspected the fence they had built. The stakes were still firmly in the ground, and the chicken wire stood tall. Most importantly, the flower shoots were still standing. The fence had worked!

Manny looked up and saw Mrs. Summers sitting on her deck. "We're almost done here, Mrs. Summers!" he said.

"That's okay, Manny!" she said,
smiling. "The berries will still be here."

When they were done with their work,
they walked to Mrs. Summers's house.

The Green Thumbs Club members soon began picking more blueberries from the bushes.

"You know, my grandma lives just two blocks away," Walter said. "I've heard her say how great it would be to plant a tree in her yard. She likes to have some shade in the summer." He dropped a few blueberries into his bucket.

"When is she going to do it?" asked Manny.

"I don't know. I think she could use some help finding the right tree seedling for her yard, preparing the soil, and planting it," said Walter.

The boys all looked at each other.

"It could be our next project," said Walter.

"It sounds like a job for the Green Thumbs Club!" said Sadiq, laughing.

GLOSSARY

admiring (ad-MIRE-ing)—looking at something with enjoyment

bloom (BLOOM)—to produce flowers

bushy (BUSH-ee)—thick

Dugsi (DHUG-see)—Islamic school

guilty (GIL-tee)—ashamed or filled with regret because you know that you've done something wrong

handiwork (HAN-dee-werk)—something that one has made or done

hijab (HE-jahb)—a head covering worn in public by some Muslim women

injury (IN-jur-ee)—damage or harm

inspected (in-SPEKT-id)—examined something carefully

marigold (MAR-ri-gohld)—a garden plant that has orange, yellow, or red flowers

measurement (MEZH-ur-muhnt)—the size, weight, or amount of something that has been measured

possibility (PAH-suh-BILL-i-tee)—a thing that may happen

Qur'an (kuh-RAHN)—the holy book of the Muslim religion

relax (ri-LAKS)—to take a rest from work or do something enjoyable

seedling (SEED-ling)—a young plant that has been grown from a seed

volunteer (vah-luhn-TEER)—to offer to do a job without pay

wheelchair (WEEL-chair)—a chair on wheels for people who are not able to walk because they are sick, injured, or disabled

wriggling (RIG-ling)—twisting or turning with quick movements

TALK ABOUT IT

1. Talk about a time that you helped someone in need. Did you want to help them? Were you glad you did?

2. At first Sadiq doesn't want to help Mr. Kassim. What clues from the text tell you why Sadiq didn't want to help?

3. Do you think that the Green Thumbs Club members are happy they helped Mr. Kassim? Discuss why or why not using clues from the text.

WRITE IT DOWN

1. Sadiq looks up to Nuurali, so when his brother suggests he help Mr. Kassim, he's convinced. Who do you look up to? Write a paragraph about that person.

2. Imagine you are part of the Green Thumbs Club. Put together a flyer advertising your gardening work.

3. Write another scene that takes places a couple of months later, when Mrs. Kassim returns from Somalia. How does she react to the garden?

MAKE A TERRARIUM

Sadiq and his friends learned about gardening from Mr. Kassim. You can learn about gardening too by making your own mini garden in a terrarium!

WHAT YOU NEED:

- glass jar with a lid
- ruler
- sand
- small pebbles
- potting soil
- small plants
- moss
- stones
- toy plants and animals
- water

WHAT TO DO:

1. Clean out the jar and let it dry.

2. Add a layer of sand (about 1 inch or 2.5 centimeters) to the bottom of the jar.

3. Add a layer of pebbles (about 1 inch or 2.5 centimeters) on top of the sand.

4. Next add a layer of potting soil (about 2 inches or 5 centimeters).

5. Plant the small plants and moss in the soil.

6. Decorate your terrarium with stones, toy plants, and toy animals if you want! A toy bunny won't eat the plants like the real ones did in Mr. Kassim's garden.

7. Water the terrarium so the sand layer at the bottom is wet.

8. Place a lid and tightly seal the terrarium jar. Place it near a window, but make sure to not put it in direct sunlight.

9. Watch the plants grow as they take care of themselves within the terrarium!

CREATORS

Siman Nuurali grew up in Kenya. She now lives in Minnesota. Siman and her family are Somali— just like Sadiq and his family! She and her five children love to play badminton and board games together. Siman works at Children's Hospital, and in her free time, she also enjoys writing and reading.

Anjan Sarkar is a British illustrator based in Sheffield, England. Since he was little, Anjan has always loved drawing stuff. And now he gets to draw stuff all day for his job. Hooray! In addition to the Sadiq series, Anjan has been drawing mischievous kids, undercover aliens, and majestic tigers for other exciting children's book projects.